Martin Bridge
Sound the Alarm!

Written by
Jessica Scott Kerrin

Illustrated by
Joseph Kelly

Kids Can Press

For Peter and Elliott, with special thanks to my mom, Mary, who inspired "Props." Thanks also to the staff of Halifax Dance, who taught me some fancy footwork along the way — J.S.K.

Per Suzi. Mia sorella ha un ombrello verde! — J.K.

Text © 2007 Jessica Scott Kerrin
Illustrations © 2007 Joseph Kelly

Kids Can Press acknowledges the financial support of the Government of Ontario, through the Ontario Media Development Corporation's Ontario Book Initiative; the Ontario Arts Council; the Canada Council for the Arts; and the Government of Canada, through the BPIDP, for our publishing activity.

Published in Canada by
Kids Can Press Ltd.
29 Birch Avenue
Toronto, ON M4V 1E2

Published in the U.S. by
Kids Can Press Ltd.
2250 Military Road
Tonawanda, NY 14150

www.kidscanpress.com

Edited by Debbie Rogosin
Designed by Julia Naimska
Printed and bound in Canada

The art in this book was drawn with graphite and charcoal; shading was added digitally.

The text is set in GarthGraphic.

The hardcover edition of this book is smyth sewn casebound.

The paperback edition of this book is limp sewn with a drawn-on cover.

CM 07 0 9 8 7 6 5 4 3 2 1
CM PA 07 0 9 8 7 6 5 4 3 2 1

Library and Archives Canada Cataloguing in Publication

Kerrin, Jessica Scott
    Martin Bridge sound the alarm! / written by Jessica Scott Kerrin ; illustrated by Joseph Kelly.

ISBN-13: 978-1-55337-976-8 (bound)   ISBN-10: 1-55337-976-4 (bound)
ISBN-13: 978-1-55337-977-5 (pbk.)   ISBN-10: 1-55337-977-2 (pbk.)

I. Kelly, Joseph II. Title.

PS8621.E77M373 2006   jC813'.6   C2006-903628-4

Kids Can Press is a _l©ſ∪s_™ Entertainment company

Contents

Meet ...

Martin

Darla

Stuart

Alex

Moon Eyes

Martin's dad was humming a familiar tune when Martin came down for breakfast. It was the theme song from *Zip Rideout: Space Cadet*, Martin's longtime favorite cartoon.

Martin joined in the humming, and then he caught on to why his dad was doing it.

"Hey! Isn't that the new Zip Rideout movie?" Martin asked. He peered at the newspaper over his dad's shoulder and pointed to an advertisement. Zip was soaring across the sky in his flaming rocket.

"Sure is," said his dad, who paused to take a long sip of coffee. "How about we go this weekend?"

Martin whooped, then sat down to pour himself an extra-large bowl of Zip Rideout Space Flakes. He ate them every morning.

"Want to come, Mom?" asked Martin between spoonfuls. But he already knew the answer. Martin's mom was not a Zip fan.

"I'll pass," she said with a chuckle. "You boys have fun."

"Can we go tonight, Dad?" asked Martin. "It's Friday."

"Not tonight," his mom cut in. "Your dad and I already have plans."

"You're going out tonight?" asked Martin. "What for?"

"It's our anniversary," said his dad,

"and I'm taking your mom to dinner."

"And dancing," said his mom. She gave his dad moon eyes, then stood to clear the dishes.

"Dancing!" repeated Martin to his dad. He made an icky face, but his dad had gone back to reading the newspaper. Martin shrugged and dug into his cereal.

"I've arranged for a new sitter," Martin's mom announced while she clattered at the sink. "Her name is Darla."

"Darla!" exclaimed Martin, setting down his spoon. "Why not Bruce?"

Bruce was his regular sitter. Whenever Bruce came over, he and Martin filled up

on potato chips and homemade milk shakes. Then they would fly paper airplanes from the top of the stairs and watch bad-guy movies until way past Martin's bedtime.

"Bruce went away to university, remember?" said his mom. "I got Darla's name from a mom at work. She comes highly recommended."

Martin groaned. He knew what that meant. Darla would be one of those sitters who thought fruit was a perfectly good snack. There would be no flying airplanes in the house, he was sure of that. And she would insist that he go to bed on time.

A real drill sergeant.

"Better get moving, Sport," said his dad, checking the wall clock. "You'll be late for the bus."

Martin looked up with a jolt. Once again, he had lost track of time. Cripes!

He ran upstairs and brushed his teeth, then grabbed his knapsack and jacket before bolting out the door.

Too late. The school bus stood waiting. Martin knew that Mrs. Phips, his cranky-pants driver, would mutter something in that gravelly voice of hers as he climbed on board.

She was grumpy, all right.

Martin made out the words "punctuality" and "thankless" as he tried to scoot by.

"Sorry, Mrs. Phips," Martin replied dutifully.

As he scrambled toward the back, he noticed that Thomas, one of the older passengers, was smirking at him.

Martin paused to look down and check himself out. He was wearing his superhero jacket like always, but it wasn't zipped up funny or anything.

Martin continued down the aisle. When

he passed by, Thomas called out sarcastically, "All systems ready, Captain?" and gave Martin a mocking Zip Rideout salute.

The older boys on either side burst out laughing.

Martin fumed. He knew perfectly well that Thomas used to love Zip Rideout. Thomas was one of the few kids who owned a complete set of Zip Rideout cereal cards, and he could act out entire scenes from Zip's television show completely from memory. But now that he was almost in junior high, Thomas made fun of anything to do with Zip — and anyone who liked the space cadet.

Martin was about to defend his superhero when Mrs. Phips hollered at them to settle down.

Martin shot Thomas a hostile glare,

then slid in beside his best friend, Stuart.
Stuart was scowling, his Zip Rideout
lunchbox tucked at his side.

"Thomas
got you, too?"
whispered
Martin. He
could feel his
ears burning.

Stuart
nodded, lips
pressed tight.

Martin
shook his

head. He *loved* his Zip Rideout jacket with
its star-shaped zipper pull, extra padding at
the elbows and badge of honor on the
front. And he thought Stuart's lunchbox

was a blast with its rocket-shaped handle and the entire galaxy painted on its side.

Martin crossed his arms. Absolutely no amount of growing up would make *him* change his mind about Zip. And with that, Martin recited the extended version of Zip's loyalty pledge in his head.

When they arrived at school, Martin and Stuart met Alex, their other best friend, at the front steps. He was sporting his Zip Rideout space goggles.

"Onwards and upwards!" said Alex. It was something Zip Rideout said at the start of every mission.

Martin and Stuart saluted Alex, and they headed inside. Martin had a good day by avoiding Thomas at recess and lunch. But on the ride home, he received another mocking salute from Thomas.

"Keep it moving!" hollered Mrs. Phips before Martin could respond.

That night, Martin went up to his room right after his mom fixed him a quick dinner. He wanted to rearrange his rocket collection, and he was halfway done when the doorbell rang.

"Martin!" his mom sang out.

"Coming," answered Martin. He sighed and trundled down the stairs into a cloud of his mom's perfume.

"Darla, this is Martin," said his mom, whose hair was all done up. Martin could see the dangly earrings his dad had given her.

"Hi there," said Darla, all breezy and smiles.

"Hi," Martin replied gruffly, both hands stuffed into his pockets.

Too bad about Bruce. He would have play-punched Martin by now.

"You look beautiful, Mrs. Bridge," cooed Darla.

"Why, thank you, Darla," said his mom, gently tugging a few curls at the back of her neck and turning to Martin.

Martin knew he should also say something nice about her, but the way his evening was shaping up made him too grumpy for that.

When Martin's mom opened the closet to hang up Darla's coat, Darla spotted Martin's jacket.

"A Zip Rideout jacket!" she said, turning to Martin.

Well now, thought Martin. It seemed that Darla knew about his superhero. Not all was lost. He began to smile, but then she continued.

"I bet it looks sweet on you."

Martin's smile collapsed. There was nothing sweet about a Zip Rideout jacket.

Martin's mom saw his face and quickly steered

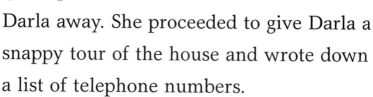

Darla away. She proceeded to give Darla a snappy tour of the house and wrote down a list of telephone numbers.

Martin's dad joined them in the

kitchen, and he whistled at Martin's mom. "Ooh la la," he said, giving her moon eyes, then winking at Martin.

Martin scuffed at the floor.

"And you must be Darla," said his dad, shaking Darla's hand.

"Nice to meet you," gushed Darla.

"Well, we'd better get going," said his dad. "Have fun, Sport."

"And be good," said Martin's mom while his dad helped with her coat. She gave Martin a loud kiss good-bye, then wiped the orange lipstick smudge from his cheek.

Martin shut the door behind them, rubbing the spot to make sure nothing was left. He turned to Darla.

"They're going dancing," he said and rolled his eyes.

"How romantic," said Darla in a breathless voice. She clasped her hands and looked up with a dreamy gaze.

Martin looked up, too. All he saw was the ceiling fan.

He decided then and there that Darla would be no fun whatsoever.

"I'll be in my room," he said and headed back upstairs before she could say anything else.

After Martin had rearranged his rocket collection just so, he lay on his bed with a smile. He was thinking about going to the new Zip Rideout movie. Then he thought about how Thomas probably wouldn't see it on account of being too old for Zip.

Cripes!

Martin rolled over. Well, it would be Thomas's loss, and too bad for him since the movie promised to be spectacular!

Martin reached over and grabbed Admiral, the furry stuffed turtle he slept with. They stared at each other. It was then that Martin noticed how the fur had worn off Admiral's cheeks.

Martin patted Admiral's head. He had had Admiral ever since he could sleep without a night-light. But now Admiral looked threadbare.

Martin gently placed the turtle on the bookshelf where he kept old toys that he wanted to save. Besides, he reasoned, he didn't need a sleeping buddy anymore. Martin was all about rockets now.

Laughter from the living room interrupted his thoughts. He slid down the railing to investigate. Surrounded by teen magazines, Darla was painting her toenails in front of the blaring television.

"Hey, Martin," she called. "My favorite show is on. Come join me."

As soon as Martin sat down, he wished he hadn't. It was one of those kissy shows that made him cringe and want to change the channel. But there were funny bits, too, so he stuck it out.

"My school's having a dance next week," said Darla in that breezy voice of hers during a commercial for shampoo.

"Hmmm," said Martin, barely answering. Even shampoo was more interesting than listening to Darla gush about some stupid junior high school dance.

"So I brought over a dance demo," she continued, unfazed. She dug so noisily through her knapsack that Martin had to turn up the volume.

"A-ha!" She held it up, blocking Martin's view of the screen.

Martin was about to ask Darla to please move over when she added, "My brothers would tease me if I practiced at home. And I really, really like to dance."

Martin paused.

He thought about Thomas, and he thought about Zip Rideout, and something inside him softened.

"You want to watch it now?" he asked with resignation.

"Oh, yes, please!" she chirped, handing the demo to him.

Martin trudged across the living room and popped it into the machine. Music began to play. Straight away, he liked it. He watched as a crowd gathered around two dancers moving to the beat.

"Ooooh! I wish I could do that. Quick, Martin! Help me move the coffee table out of the way," said Darla.

Martin lifted his end and they carried the table to one side.

Once the dance floor was clear, Darla began to practice. Martin returned to his chair, half watching her, half watching the screen and picking at his fingernails all the while.

"Rats," said Darla. She kept messing up.

"You're doing it wrong," remarked Martin, head now resting on his hand. "It's your feet," he added.

"What do you mean?" puffed Darla.

Martin got up to replay the demo. "See his feet," said Martin, pointing to the screen. "They go: Front. Side. Then cross, cross, tap."

"Front. Side. Cross, cross, tap," said Darla, trying again. But she still couldn't do it.

"Front. Side. Cross, cross, tap," Martin instructed as he

tried the move himself. Only it was harder than it looked. "Hang on," said Martin, more to himself than to Darla, and he repeated the steps.

It was the *cross, cross* part that was tricky. But Darla cheered him on, so he kept trying.

"Martin!" Darla exclaimed at last. "You're doing it!"

Martin performed the whole dance move again for good measure. It felt great.

"If you keep this up," Darla continued, "all the girls will want to dance with you!"

Martin froze, suddenly aware of what he was doing. Dancing!

Alarm bells went off in his head.

He plunked onto the sofa, arms crossed, ears burning.

"Hey, Martin," said Darla. "I didn't mean

anything by that. It's
just, well, girls like
guys who can dance."

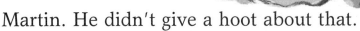

"Cripes," muttered
Martin. He didn't give a hoot about that.

Darla gave him a long, sideways look,
then ejected the dance demo from the
machine. She settled on the sofa and began
to flip through the television channels.

Click. Click. Click.

"There!" said Martin eagerly.

Zip Rideout: Space Cadet lit the screen.

"Zip it is," she said quietly.

They watched for a bit until Martin's
ears returned to normal.

"Say, Martin," said Darla, all gushiness
gone. "I bet *someday* you'll want to learn a
few more dance moves."

"I don't think so," said Martin firmly, keeping his eyes glued to his show. "I like rockets."

"Well, if you do change your mind," said Darla gently, "you can always borrow my dance demo. Here." She handed him a piece of paper. It had her name and telephone number written on it. "Just give me a call."

"Sure," said Martin without interest. He held the paper awkwardly and returned to the show. Zip Rideout had just discovered the lost planet of Astro.

"I've seen this one before," said Martin. "He meets his archenemy, Crater Man, for the very first time."

"I know," said Darla. "And Zip frees the Astronians from Crater Man's evil grip."

"You've seen this one, too?"

"Sure," said Darla. "I've seen all the *Zip* shows. I think I still have a Zip Rideout poster plastered somewhere in my room."

Martin turned to her in amazement.

"Wow!" he said. "I've got an almost complete set of Zip Rideout cereal cards."

"Let's see them!" said Darla. Her

gushiness had returned, but somehow it was less annoying.

Martin raced to the front closet and hauled out his jacket. He pulled the cards from his pocket, shoved Darla's paper in,

then rushed back to the living room. He proceeded to lay the cards on the coffee table in their groupings while Darla picked up individual ones for closer inspection.

"Zip's first rocket. Wow! This card is rare."

Martin nodded proudly, then allowed her time to  admire each and every one before scooping up his collection. "Say, do you want me to make us some milk shakes? I know how."

Martin had not made them by himself before, but he had helped Bruce plenty of times.

"That would be great," said Darla, and they headed to the kitchen. "I'm thirsty after all that dancing."

It took a while to gather the ingredients and clean up the mess, but the milk shakes  were delicious. Darla and Martin were just finishing up when they spotted headlights in the driveway.

"Quick, Martin!" she said, sounding the alarm. "It's way past your bedtime!"

"I'll show you my rocket collection next time," he promised as he flew up the stairs.

With only seconds to spare, Martin jumped into his pajamas and slid between his sheets with their pattern of orbiting satellites.

After clickety-clacking up the stairs, his mom peeked in to check on him. Martin breathed deeply as if he was sleeping, until she gently closed the door behind her.

"Good night, Admiral," he whispered. Then he rolled over and fell asleep, dance music still playing in his head.

"So, how was Darla?" asked Martin's dad merrily at breakfast as he cracked some eggs.

"She's all right," said Martin, pouring his Zip Rideout Space Flakes.

"What did you two do?"

"Watched television," said Martin, "and stuff."

Best not to mention the dancing, he thought as he added the milk. His dad seemed too playful this morning, and Martin wasn't up for any teasing.

Martin reached for his spoon as his mom twirled into the kitchen. Her housecoat billowed around her.

39

"Good morning, lamb chop," his dad
said as he placed breakfast in front of her.

They exchanged moon eyes.

Martin dug noisily into his cereal to
break the mood. "How was your evening?"

he asked between mouthfuls.

"We had a lovely time," said his mom happily. "Your dad is quite the dancer. He remembers all the moves."

"Darla is going to a dance," Martin remarked.

"Well, yes. She is in junior high, after all," said his mom.

"I don't see what the big deal is."

"Oh, it *is* a big deal. You'll see. Someday." She leaned over to kiss him on the forehead.

"I like rockets," said Martin firmly. And then he remembered that he and his dad were going to see Zip's new film. "What time is the movie?" Martin asked.

"Two o'clock," said his dad. And they both started to hum Zip's theme song.

Zip Rideout: All Systems Ready turned out to be the best movie Martin had ever seen. Intergalactic aliens. H_2O Faster Blasters. Earth-shattering explosions.

Best of all, no kissing.

"How about some ice cream?" asked his dad as they were leaving the theater.

"Roger!" said Martin, like his superhero. And Martin was in such a good mood, he said "Roger" as much as he could for the rest of the weekend.

On Monday morning, as Martin finished his usual breakfast, he looked up at the wall clock.

"I'd better get moving," he announced.

"Well! That's a first!" exclaimed his dad.

"What do you mean?" asked Martin, bringing his dishes to the sink.

"I didn't have to remind you about the bus," said his dad, ruffling Martin's hair.

Martin shrugged modestly. It was true. For once, he wouldn't be late.

"You're on time," observed Mrs. Phips as Martin climbed aboard. "Fancy that!"

"Roger," replied Martin, giving her a wink. But his face fell when he spotted Thomas ready to pounce with his tired one-liner.

"All systems ready, Captain?" Thomas taunted in that annoying tone of his.

"Settle down back there!" was Mrs. Phips's immediate response.

Martin shifted his knapsack higher on his shoulder and kept walking. A piece of paper fluttered from his jacket pocket.

"What's this?" Thomas called as he plucked the paper from the floor.

Martin turned to see what Thomas had.

It was Darla's name and telephone number, written in her girly writing.

Thomas looked up, eyes wide. "You have Darla McGonagle's number?" he asked in amazement. "*The* Darla McGonagle?"

Martin shrugged.

"What are *you* doing with *her* number?"

The others stared at Martin,  jaws agape.

"She gave it to me," said Martin matter-of-factly. "On Friday night," he added.

Jaws dropped even farther.

"Friday night?" repeated Thomas in amazement.

"Sure," said Martin. "Right after we danced." He snatched the note back.

There was total silence on the bus.

A sea of passengers stared at Martin in
awe. Even Mrs. Phips turned around.

At first he couldn't figure out why.
And then he understood.

Oh, thought Martin.

A slow smile spread across his face.

Martin stood tall. "Darla says girls *like* guys who can dance," he boasted. And right there in the aisle he performed the dance move he had learned.

Flawlessly. *Front. Side. Cross, cross, tap. Front. Side. Cross, cross, tap.*

With that, he sauntered to the back and sat

beside Stuart. The bus pulled out.

"By the way," Martin called to Thomas. "Do you know who else Darla likes?"

Thomas gave the tiniest shake of his head.

"Zip Rideout," declared Martin, pointing to his jacket with both thumbs.

Silence returned as Thomas slunk down even farther into his seat. Then murmurs began to fill the bus.

Stuart chuckled and placed his Zip Rideout lunchbox proudly on his lap.

"Well," said Martin. "I guess he won't be making fun of Zip anymore." He tucked Darla's telephone number back into his pocket and gave it a pat.

"Sure," said Stuart. "But now you've got a whole new problem."

"What do you mean?" asked Martin. He looked up in alarm.

Every single girl had turned around to stare at him. And each one wore the same soft expression.

Moon eyes.

Props

Martin waited for his eyes to get used to the gloom before moving further inside the props shed that stood in Stuart's backyard.

Usually it was locked. But today, Stuart had the key.

The props shed was packed to the rafters with all kinds of stuff. Colossal dragonfly wings, marching penguins, a suit of armor, a giant beanstalk, a red go-cart, a disco ball.

"Watch out for spiders," said Stuart,

imitating his mom's voice. He chuckled.
"Mom always says that. Spiders give her
the creeps."

"Your mom has the best job in the
world," Martin marveled, ignoring the
spider warning and taking a small step
forward. He reached up and gently touched
the pink flamingo hanging above him. It
started to twirl in slow motion.

Stuart's mom made stage sets for the Velvet Curtain Theater. In between plays, she often decorated display windows for department stores. She was so good, crowds would stop on the sidewalk to watch her as she worked on her creations behind the glass.

"Mom said to look near the plastic campfire," said Stuart matter-of-factly. For Stuart, there was nothing unusual about having a mother who made magic or a props shed in his backyard filled with theatrical leftovers.

At first, Martin had been annoyed when Stuart's mom called, interrupting their water-sprinkler game. She was working on a window for a store called The Toy Box, and she had forgotten to bring the remote control for her robotic dolphin.

But now Martin nodded to Stuart, eager for the chance to rummage through the shed. Shoving aside a bicycle built for two, he wormed his way past a pile of overstuffed sheep, then squeezed around a roly-poly punching-bag clown.

Good thing Stuart's on the other side of the shed, thought Martin. Stuart hated clowns.

Martin was thoroughly enjoying his romp through wonderland and hoped they wouldn't find the remote control any time soon.

Then he gasped.

"What's wrong?" asked Stuart, his voice muffled by a rack of fairy tutus.

"Nothing!" choked Martin. He struggled

to push back his mounting panic, but he was unable to look away from the thing he feared the most.

Not a spider. He liked things with eight legs.

Not the clown. He liked happy-go-lucky characters.

No, it was a mannequin. Lurking in the nearby corner. Staring straight at him with those cold, unfeeling eyes. Reaching out to touch him with those stiff, plastic fingers. Screaming silent words at him with that half-open mouth.

Martin couldn't breathe. His palms started to sweat. He swallowed hard, then frantically shoved his way back out, all the while fighting the prickly feeling that the mannequin was in hot pursuit.

To Martin, mannequins were the most loathsome things on earth. He had nightmares about them. And even though he knew they couldn't possibly move in real life, Martin was absolutely convinced they did.

But only when he wasn't looking.

"Found it!" called Stuart happily from somewhere deep inside the shed.

By now, Martin was safely outside, taking slow, deep breaths. Stuart emerged, remote control in hand.

"You okay?" he asked, a puzzled frown on his face.

"Yes," said Martin shakily, hands on knees. But he stood up to stop Stuart from asking any more embarrassing questions.

"Let's go."

Stuart gave him a funny look, then locked the shed. Martin double-checked it to make sure the mannequin couldn't escape. He felt better after that.

The boys jumped on their bikes and headed to The Toy Box, six blocks away. Only it was getting close to dinner. Martin could tell because his stomach was growling. He decided he would run the errand with Stuart, then head straight home.

They wheeled into the parking lot. It was full of cars and scattered shopping carts. As they pedaled by the onlookers, the boys waved to Stuart's mom in the second-floor window. Martin got a quick glimpse of the underwater scene she was building to go with the water toys displayed in the first-floor window.

"The bike rack is at the side," Stuart called over his shoulder.

They locked their bikes together, then headed through the front doors of the store.

The Toy Box was so big, it had two floors. Little kid stuff on the main floor. Big kid stuff upstairs, along with the magnificent display window Martin had seen from outside.

"This way," said Stuart.

They climbed the stairs and then marched to the window, which was blocked off from the rest of the store by panels.

"Abracadabra," said Stuart as he knocked on one of the panels.

A hidden door opened, and his mom climbed out.

"One remote," reported Stuart, handing it to her.

"Thank you, honey." She glanced at her watch. "Oh, no! I'm really behind, and I have to get this window done before the store closes. As soon as you get home, will you please remind your dad to start dinner?"

"Sure," said Stuart.

Suddenly, she screeched and dropped the remote. "Is that what I think it is?!"

The boys took a step closer and inspected the remote. A small spider crept across the control buttons.

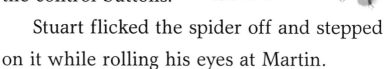

Stuart flicked the spider off and stepped on it while rolling his eyes at Martin.

Stuart's mom gave him a quick kiss. Then she grabbed the remote, climbed back into the window display and shut the door.

"You weren't kidding. She really *does* hate spiders," said Martin.

"I know," said Stuart. "It's silly. It's not like they're *clowns* or anything."

Martin was about to tell him that being scared of clowns was even sillier. But then he remembered his own peculiar fear of mannequins, so he said nothing.

Stuart turned and surveyed the second floor. "Want to look around for a minute while we're here?"

Martin's stomach rumbled again. But still, they *were* standing inside a toy store, the biggest in the city. He couldn't resist.

"Let's check out the Zip Rideout aisle," Martin suggested.

Zip Rideout: Space Cadet was their favorite cartoon show. Zip had become so popular, he now had an entire aisle of merchandise all to himself. Rocket kits,

space goggles, H₂O Faster Blasters, Solar
System Explorer Sets, movie posters,
lunchboxes, jackets, watches. Even
pajamas, sheets and toothbrushes!

The boys bounded across the store,
dodging noisy swarms of kids. They cut
through the puzzles and games aisle, which
was empty except for a few grandparents,
then past the bicycles and the
all-pink girly aisle.

The next aisle was for action figures.

"Getting close," said Stuart with authority.

They turned the corner, and there it was. The Zip Rideout aisle.

"Ready and steady," said Martin, giving Stuart the official Zip Rideout salute.

The boys zigzagged their way down the

aisle, trying space toy after space toy. They were having a blast, but stopped in their tracks when they came to the end of the row.

There, looming in front of them, stood an enormous model of Zip Rideout's rocket. It had Zip's signature flames painted in blazing reds and oranges with the name of Zip's rocket in bold letters: "The Zipper."

"Look! There's even a hatch door," said Martin, fully impressed. "Let's climb on board."

"I don't know," said Stuart hesitantly. "Maybe we're not allowed."

"But that's what a hatch door is for!" insisted Martin. "And we could act out episode twenty-four: 'Zip Rideout and the Wormhole.'"

Martin knew episode twenty-four was Stuart's all-time favorite.

A wave of excited anticipation crossed Stuart's face. "You first," he ordered.

Martin pried open the hatch as fast as the speed of light. Stuart clambered in right behind him.

"Wow!" exclaimed Martin, looking around. There were flashing control panels and maps of galaxies and everything.

He closed the hatch door and all was silent. Just like being in a real spaceship. The two acted out the entire wormhole episode, with the crash landing from episode sixteen thrown in for good measure.

When they were done, Martin sat at the helm, enjoying the starry view on the screen above.

"I'd give anything to have The Zipper
in my backyard," he said wistfully. The
thought of home made his stomach start
up again. It must be getting late.

"We'd better get going," agreed Stuart,
rubbing his own stomach.

And that's when the lights inside the
rocket went out, plunging the boys into
total darkness.

"Quit fooling around," said Stuart.

"It wasn't me," insisted Martin.
"Someone must have pulled the plug."

He began to grope the walls in search
of the hatch door. The blackness pressed
against him, and the boys kept bumping
into each other as
they fumbled about.

"Here's the hatch,"
said Martin at last,
feeling something
familiar. He twisted
the handle and
pushed the door
wide open.

They poked their heads out.

"What's going on?" whispered Martin.

The store lights were also off. And everything was as silent as it had been inside the rocket.

"I think the store is closed," Stuart whispered back. "H-h ... hello?" he called tentatively.

No answer.

They scrambled away from the rocket and stood uncertainly in the dim, vacant aisle.

"Let's get out of here!" urged Martin, and they wove their way back to the stairs.

It was Martin who first noticed that an accordion-type gate had been pulled across the top of the stairwell. It reached from floor to ceiling. Stuart tried to slide it open, but it wouldn't budge.

"It's locked," said Stuart in a shocked tone.

"Let me try," said Martin. He rattled the gate several times.

Nothing.

He looked at Stuart, and Stuart looked at him.

Cripes!

"Now what?!" said Stuart, his voice several notches higher than usual.

"A telephone!" said Martin. "Let's call for help!"

"The telephones are downstairs by the front doors!" Stuart wailed. Like Martin, he pressed his face to the gate, clinging to it with both hands.

"Okay, okay," said Martin. Stuart's rising alarm was beginning to get to him. "We'll have to think of something else. Go to Plan B."

"Which is?" demanded Stuart, keeping his grip on the gate.

"Which is for you to be quiet so I can think," said Martin irritably.

He glanced over at Stuart, who now looked so distraught that Martin immediately felt bad.

"Sorry," he mumbled. "Let's go sit down and figure this out."

Stuart followed Martin to the car aisle. Martin sat in

a push-pedal convertible. Stuart chose a station wagon with fake wood-paneled doors.

They parked in silence.

"Wait a minute!" Martin shouted. "Our bikes! Someone will spot them and realize that we're trapped in here!"

"Our bikes are locked up around the side," said Stuart glumly, forehead on steering wheel. "Remember?"

"Oh," said Martin. "Right." His voice trailed off.

Suddenly, Stuart sat up tall, eyes wide open.

"The clowns!" he squeezed out. "The *clowns!*"

"What?" asked Martin, confused at the outburst.

"Which aisle are the clowns in?" Stuart dropped his voice to a whisper, as if he feared being overheard by them.

"Ah!" Now Martin understood. "Clowns are downstairs, next to the birthday party aisle. Not up *here*," he said reassuringly.

Stuart sagged with relief.

The mention of clowns reminded Martin about his own fear. But since this wasn't a clothing store, he was happily sure that there weren't any mannequins lurking around. Good thing, since he had had a nightmare about them only a few sleeps ago.

Still, he didn't like the idea of spending the entire night in The Toy Box.

Not one bit.

Then he spotted the display of Park Ranger Super-Charged All-Night Flashlights. It gave him a fabulous idea.

"We won't be here for long," said Martin triumphantly. "We're going to *signal* for help."

"Signal?" repeated Stuart, hope creeping into his voice. "How?"

"With one of these," said Martin,
climbing out of the car and picking up a
flashlight from the display. "We'll beam
a light from the window. I know how
to signal S-O-S, which means 'help.'
Someone's bound to see us."

"That might work," said Stuart cautiously.

"Except Park Ranger Super-Charged All-Night Flashlights never come with batteries. And they need a gazillion, don't they?"

"No problem," said Martin, now thinking on his feet. "All we need to do is visit the battery aisle."

"Bingo!" exclaimed Stuart. He slapped Martin on the back.

They dashed over to the battery aisle

and inserted a fistful into the flashlight. Martin switched it on. It worked!

"Let's get to the window," he said eagerly.

They ran back to the wall of panels that covered the underwater scene Stuart's mom had been working on. Stuart pushed open the hidden door and they climbed inside.

Martin froze.

It was very dark.

Too dark for a window.

Martin flashed his light to where the window was and discovered that the bottom half was now painted with starfish and seaweed. He slowly slid the beam up the window. Above their heads, the glass turned clear.

But that wasn't what made Martin scream.

"What?!! What?!!" yelled Stuart, charging for the door without bothering to wait for an answer.

"Mannequins!" Martin choked out. The beam of his flashlight shook violently. Martin's recurring nightmare was coming true!

Stuart poked his head back in and

looked up. Above them, mannequin
children in bathing suits swam and dove in
the painted water scene. A robotic dolphin
frolicked alongside them, its tail turned off
in mid-flick.

Stuart climbed back into the display
area and stood beside Martin, surveying
the scene above.

"Are you worried that the mannequins will fall on us?" asked Stuart. "Because I'm pretty sure my mom would have tied them up well."

Martin couldn't say anything because his throat was squeezed tight with terror. Instead, he slowly backed out of the window display, keeping a constant eye on the mannequins in case any of them tried to follow.

"Martin? Where are you going?" demanded Stuart, trailing behind the shaking flashlight beam all the way back to the top of the stairs.

Martin pressed against the gate. But there was no escape.

"Here's the thing," he huffed, doubling over, hands on knees once again. "I hate mannequins."

"You hate mannequins?" repeated Stuart. "Why?"

"Why? I don't know why! Why does your mom hate spiders? Why do you hate clowns?"

Stuart thought a minute. "Well, I don't know about spiders, but clowns? Come on! That frilly thing they wear around their neck? Those really big feet? That honking sound they make? What's to like?"

Martin thrust the flashlight at Stuart. "Fine. *You* signal. I'll wait here."

"But I don't know S-O-S."

"It's three short bursts, three long, three short. Then keep repeating the whole thing."

"But they're just *mannequins*," Stuart persisted.

Martin shot him his very best death glare.

"Oh, all right," said Stuart gruffly. He grabbed the flashlight and climbed back inside the window display.

Martin stood with his arms tightly wrapped around himself.

Less than a minute later, Stuart returned. "It's no use," he said. "The paint on the window is blocking the flashlight beam. You'll have to boost me up so I can shine the signal out the top where the glass is clear."

"No," said Martin flatly. "I *won't* go back in there."

But then Stuart said something really mean. "So, you're okay spending the night with mannequins? They're locked in with us on *this* side, you know." He shook the gate for chilling emphasis.

No response from Martin. Stuart's comment had turned his knees to pudding. He sat down beside the gate.

Stuart plunked down beside him.

"Come on, Martin. We need to work together to get out of this one," he said sincerely.

Martin shook his head, and Stuart sighed. They sat there for a long, long time. Finally, Stuart spoke again.

"Hey, Martin. Shine the light on my hands."

"What?"

"Go on. Do it."

Martin shone the beam while Stuart twisted his fingers to cast a shadow that looked like a spider crawling up the wall.

"Your mom would hate that," observed

Martin, not amused. He handed the
flashlight back.

That got Martin thinking about his mom
and how nothing much frightened her.

In fact, she often told Martin that the
only thing she feared was
losing *him*. She
said so because
when Martin
was little, he
had once gotten
lost during
a downtown
shopping trip.
Martin never liked recalling
that event, but now, stuck here in the
empty toy store, that haunting memory
rushed back to him in vivid detail.

He remembered he had frantically charged up and down the aisles looking for his mom, until finally he had spotted the back of her coat as she stood in the women's jacket department. He darted up from behind and grabbed her hand in relief.

Only her hand was cold and stiff, and when it fell to the floor, several fingers snapped off.

He had grabbed hold of a mannequin wearing the exact same coat as his mom!

Martin's nonstop screams rang out through the entire store, bringing not only his mom, but six others to the rescue.

Yet, as frightening as that had been for Martin, it was his mom who had cried while she hugged him, then again when she later told the story to his dad.

"What a nightmare!" she had sobbed over and over.

Martin's stomach complained some more. It must be way past dinner. And he still wasn't home. Would his mom be crying now?

Yes, he told himself sadly.

Martin got up. He finally understood why he hated mannequins so much, and now he knew what he had to do.

Martin took a deep breath. And another. And another.

"Okay," he said a bit shakily. "Let's do it."

"Great!" exclaimed Stuart, leaping to his feet. "You boost me and I'll signal."

"No," said Martin as evenly as he could. "Let's do it the other way around."

"Me boost you?" asked Stuart. "But

you'll be closer to the —" Stuart paused and pointed up with quick jabs.

The thought of his head near all those mannequins gave Martin a fresh wave of the willies. But he shook it off.

"Signaling will keep me busy," Martin explained.

He grabbed the flashlight before he could change his mind, and they climbed back into the window display.

"Ready and steady?" Stuart asked in a bold Zip Rideout voice.

"Onwards and upwards," Martin replied, and Stuart boosted him.

Martin rose above the painted window scene and could see clearly into the empty parking lot. He began to signal.

Three short bursts, three long, three short. Three short bursts, three long, three short. Three short bursts, three long, three short.

And all the while, he pushed away any nightmarish thoughts of the mannequins that were floating a hair's breadth above him.

It felt as if he had been
signaling forever when he spotted two people
strolling along the far sidewalk. He turned
his beam right on them. They stopped.

"I think someone sees us!" Martin
cried out.

He signaled madly and banged on the
glass.

"Help! Help!" yelled Stuart from below.

When the couple crossed the empty parking lot and got really close, Martin turned off his flashlight and waved furiously. They waved back. Then one stayed put while the other dashed away to get help.

"We're saved!" said Martin with relief.

Not long after, someone opened the main doors to the store and flicked on the lights. It was blinding.

"We're here! We're here!" called the boys, rattling the gate.

The store manager and two police officers strode across the main floor and up the stairs to where the boys stood prisoners.

"Stuart!" exclaimed the manager, unlocking the gate. "Oh, my! Your mother must be worried sick!"

One officer radioed the police station to report that they had found the missing boys. The other officer took notes as the boys told their story.

"Why didn't you sound the alarm?" he asked, looking up from his writing.

"What alarm?" the boys asked together.

The officer pointed to a fire alarm on the wall nearby, clearly visible now that the lights were on.

"Oh," the boys said sheepishly.

"Still, it was good thinking to signal at the window," said the manager.

"They're smart boys, all right," said the officer taking notes. "I'll put that in my report."

The boys beamed.

When they left the store, Martin and Stuart retrieved their bikes. Then they climbed into the backseat of the police cruiser while one of the officers loaded the bikes into the trunk.

"Want to hear the siren, boys?" the other officer asked jovially as he turned around to face them.

They nodded eagerly.

Wee-woo! Wee-woo! went the siren. Martin's heart jumped at the short, shrill bursts of sound.

It was then that Martin realized he was glad he and Stuart hadn't sounded the alarm back in the store. After all, if they had, he would still be afraid of mannequins.

Martin squared his shoulders proudly at that thought.

Stuart was dropped off first. His parents were pacing on the porch when the cruiser pulled up. The police officers let Stuart out, and he bolted across the lawn. Martin saw lots of hugging.

Then they drove to Martin's house. When they turned into the driveway, he saw that his mom and dad were waiting on the front steps. They leapt to their feet.

"Looks like *their* nightmare is over," said the officer who was driving.

"Mine, too," said Martin as he bounded out of the cruiser. "Mine, too," he repeated with conviction.

Be a Pilot!

Bruce taught Martin how to make a paper airplane that really soars! You can make one, too. Just don't aim it at your friend, your pet or your grandmother's favorite vase!

1 Fold a 22 cm by 28 cm (8 1/2 in. by 11 in.) sheet of paper in half the long way. Open out and flatten.

2 Make a 1 cm (1/2 in.) fold along the top of the sheet. Then fold over and over six more times. This will make a thick, heavy front edge.

3 Fold the two corners of the front edge into the center fold line.

4 Fold in half along the center fold line and crease.

5 Fold each wing down from the center along the angled fold line.

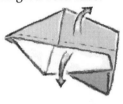

6 Push the wings up into position.

7 Glue short bits of blue wool along the tail edge for that roaring jet engine look!

Scare Yourself!

Stuart showed Martin a hand shadow sure to make Stuart's mom scream! Now Martin has come up with two scary hand shadows of his own. To try them, all you need are a small lamp (take off the shade) and a light-colored wall for a screen. Remember to stand between the lamp and the wall. And when you're done scaring yourself, make Martin's favorite animal.

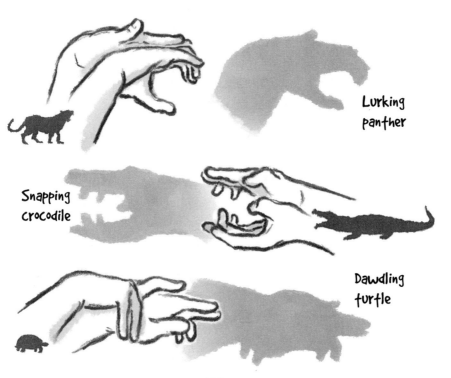

Lurking panther

Snapping crocodile

Dawdling turtle

Jessica Scott Kerrin grew up with an astronaut hero, too, but her fear of small spaces put her plans for rocket travel out of orbit. She lives with her family in Halifax, Nova Scotia, and only sounds the alarm when she sees a spider.

As head of the Bug Relocation Program at his home in Sonoma, California, **Joseph Kelly** is always ready to leap into action with a juice glass and a sheet of paper whenever his family sounds the spider alarm.

More Martin!

Martin Bridge **Ready for Takeoff!**

It was Martin's idea to decorate the
model rocket with flames. So why
did his best friend steal the idea?

HC ISBN-13: 978-1-55337-688-0
PB ISBN-13: 978-1-55337-772-6

Martin Bridge **On the Lookout!**

Martin is all set for a field trip to
the dinosaur exhibit at the museum
when the bus leaves without him!

HC ISBN-13: 978-1-55337-689-7
PB ISBN-13: 978-1-55337-773-3

Martin Bridge **Blazing Ahead!**

When Martin finds himself on
the receiving end of his friend's
pranks, it's payback time!

HC ISBN-13: 978-1-55337-961-4
PB ISBN-13: 978-1-55337-962-1

Written by Jessica Scott Kerrin   *Illustrated by* Joseph Kelly

Blast off with more chapter books from Kids Can Press

The first intergalactic spaceship ever — and it's made of cardboard!

Alex may be the inventor of the ultimate cardboard spaceship, but with a meddling little brother like Jonathan (the most annoying brother in the universe), can he ever hope to have a successful mission?

HCJ ISBN-13: 978-1-55337-886-0   PB ISBN-13: 978-1-55337-887-7

The cardboard genius defies gravity!

Despite a few setbacks — courtesy of his pesky little brother Jonathan — nothing can stop Alex now. His totally rebuilt cardboard spaceship is an improvement on the old one. And his latest invention, the Gravity Buster, is finally ready. Soon, Alex will be able to master gravity and make it do anything he wants!

HCJ ISBN-13: 978-1-55453-068-7   PB ISBN-13: 978-1-55453-069-4

Written and illustrated by Frank Asch